Mary Towle

Where is Heaven?

Mary Towle

Where is Heaven?

ISBN/EAN: 9783743369092

Manufactured in Europe, USA, Canada, Australia, Japa

Cover: Foto ©Andreas Hilbeck / pixelio.de

Manufactured and distributed by brebook publishing software
(www.brebook.com)

Mary Towle

Where is Heaven?

Where is Heaven?
and other Poems

Mary L. W. Fowle

"Earth is crammed with heaven, and every bush aflame with God."
Browning

SAN FRANCISCO

THE BANCROFT COMPANY

1890

ISSUED FROM THE PRESS OF
THE BANCROFT COMPANY
(

DEDICATION

While bringing in the sheaves of an eventful life, I catch the echo of a long silent voice, deep in tenderness and fervent in love. I see a face, radiant with spiritual beauty, reflecting the image of the heavenly in serenity, repose and rapture.

Into this sacred presence I come, with my little drift of song, and lay it at the feet of my mother.

Sorrow and joy have their free masonry, and by its sacred signs and symbols the author herewith clasps hands with all who, like herself, are standing where the shadows have fallen, waiting for the morning.

Many of these poems were first published in the New York "Illustrated Christian Weekly," and afterwards appeared in the "Christian Advocate" of the Pacific Coast, and in "Words and Work," a London publication.

"Death is the veil which they who live, call life;
We sleep, and the veil is lifted."

CONTENTS

Where is Heaven?

THIS home of the soul, is it shadowed forth
   In apocalyptic dream?
How and when can we reach the City of God,
   And bridge the dividing stream?

Does it overarch the concave blue
   Just beyond our mortal sight?
Has some one built it with beautiful hands,
   And carved its pillars of light?

Oh, where are its streams, flowing cool and still,
   Like the measure of a psalm?
And whence its bright waters, which ebb and flow,
   In the hush of endless calm?

Will those whose hearts have grown saintly and pure
   'Neath the crosses which they bore,
Just ferry us over with empty hands,
   And hearts, to the further shore?

What then? Will we find a heaven prepared
   For us who have brought no sheaves?
In time of the harvest, what of the trees
   Bearing naught—nothing but leaves?—

The heaven we make as we journey on,
   Our foretaste here below,
Is to do the will of the blessed Christ,
   And to build it as we go.

9

To be the cup of strength to the weak,
  To the fallen and the lost,
To calm the storm which has well nigh engulphed
  Some soul that is tempest-tossed,

Is to catch the breezes which play across
  The rivers which have their rise
In the hills of God, and the near behest
  Of a promised paradise.—

Thrice blest is the man, who thoughtless of self,
  Pulls strong and brave at the oar,
Which rescues a life from floods of despair
  While bearing it safe to shore.

The angels applaud! He builds as he goes
  A heaven so pure and sweet,
That the shores immortal come even here,
  Adown to his very feet.

Sutro Heights

One of the prize poems accepted by ADOLPH SUTRO, ESQ., and by him assigned a place in his archives.

HEN the old prophets taught of God
Made their sublimest flights,
Spreading their tents on table lands
Or on the mountain heights,
They caught the visions which are born
Of nearness to the sky,
As on the strong, eternal hills
Which mountains typify.

So we, of California,
Pledged to as lofty flights,
Now fix our point of vision from
The domes of " Sutro Heights."
The poetry of curves which form
The base of earth and sky,
Rocks soft the cradle which responds
To Sutro's lullaby.

Around her galleries and aisles
The rarest flowers are wreathed
Her models, frescoes, palisades,
The ages have bequeathed.
Her monuments and sacred fanes
O'erlook the sea and land,
Her tessellated pavements ring
To echo her command.

The distant hills with coronal
And valleys sweet between,
Touched by the sunset, gleam and glow
In gold and silver sheen.
Her lengthened sea beach, stretching like
A ribbon on the sand;
Defines the line which separates
Old ocean from the land.

POEMS

Behold a vision! given of God
To those who stand and wait!
Neptune, with rod and trident, now
Throws wide the Golden Gate—
We look again from " Sutro Heights "
Across the sea and land,
And catch in panoramic view
The picturesque and grand.

Mt. "Tamalpais," with gorge and scar .
Leans close against the sky;
Mount of Transfiguration! whence
We fain would mount and fly—
Sutro by night! under the stars,
Raised to a height sublime.
Reaches illimitable range
Beyond the shores of time.

Oh, when the bas-relief breaks up
And human visions fail,
We'll pass beyond these mountain heights
To those behind the veil.

The Mother's Touch

"For angels are less tenderwise than God and mothers."

—Browning.

I KNOW not how the passing years
  Have made me old to-day,
Or when they changed my sunny hair
  To sombre shades of gray;
    How strange it seems
    That sunset gleams
Fall now across my way!

Though many years have flown since I,
  By toys and dreams beguiled,
Sat in the firelight of my home,
  A loved and loving child,
    With flame more bright
    And heart more light
Because my mother smiled,

As then it thrills me now to feel,
  Adown the waste of years,
The magic of my mother's touch
  Which wiped my childhood's tears!
    Oh, gentle hand,
    With fairy wand;
It scatters all my fears.

13

My griefs and cares are soothed to-night
  While in her arms caressed,
While resting as of old my head
  Upon her faithful breast.
    The wandering dove,
    For mother-love,
  Flies to the dear home-nest.

Her fingers toying with my curls,
  Timed to some tender lay,
Beguile the years of half the pains
  Which burden them to-day.
    Oh, tender touch!
    Never was such
  On sunny hair or gray.

Blest memory, while unfolding now
  The pages of the past,
Give me of all thy valued store
  The very best thou hast.
    Oh, mother-love,
    O'ershadowing dove,
  Thy watchful vigils keep,
    While as a little child again
  I lay me down to sleep!

Threnody

TWO little lives came into ours.
    When all our hopes were young;
'Twas then we felt the blessedness
    Of wedded joys begun.
Two precious boys, linked to our hearts,
    By cords so firmly bound,
We knew not that one circlet more
    Would make the perfect round.

Ah then, when the full harmony
    Was voiceful and complete!
When soft upon our ears there fell
    The sound of Gracie's feet,
We knew our chain was perfected;
    Our little blue-eyed girl,
Clasped the third link about our hearts—
    The clasping like a pearl.

We wondered if, half we believed
    The little winsome thing,
Had come to us from Paradise
    On filmy, gauzy wing.
As bird or flower she seemed to be,
    Like incense in the air,
A presence redolent of sweet
    About us everywhere.

We knew not that this bird of ours
    Would falter on the wing,
Or that the voice that thrilled us so
    Would sometime cease to sing;
We did not think its silken nest,
    Guarded with jealous eyes,
Would let the little fledging slip
    So soon into the skies;

15

Or that our op'ning violet,
  With sweet and timid grace,
Could feel the touch of cold and storm
  Within its sheltered place.
*   *   *   *   *   *   *
  Fain would we close the door which leads
Into a chamber fair,
  Whose oft embellishment has been
Our daily tender care.
  An unpressed pillow, now as smooth
And spotless as before,
  Reflects the sunshine woven in
The carpet on the floor.

  Nature strikes not one minor key,
Because we are so sad;
  No sweet-voiced bird goes soaring by
On wings less free and glad.
  Alas, our eyes are flooded oft
With tears we cannot dry,
  Because the little feet we loved
Come no more tripping by.

  Grant thou, O Father, we may know,
The blessedness at last
  Of entering the shining gate
Through which her feet have passed;
  And that the lamp which she has set
Within the window far,
  May light us through the wilderness,
Our fixed and guiding star.

The Street Gamin

WHO is this vagrant child clogging the way,
Looking so pitiful, where does he stay?
Who owns the graceless lad, with garments torn,
Looking so desolate, gaunt and forlorn?

Where does he stay when nights fold darkly in?
What shelter harbors him from want and sin?
Who waits to welcome him 'round the warm hearth,
Where loving voices blend in household mirth?

Where is his mother now, patient and sweet?
Looking with wistful eyes out on the street?
Or with her loving hands placing some toy
Just where she knows 'twill please her truant boy?

Who rounds his little bed with tender care?
Who holds his childish hands, lifted in prayer?
Who soothes his boyish griefs, wiping each tear,
Calling him treasured names, tender and dear?

Nobody's boy; alas! nobody's child;
Out in the wilderness barren and wild,
Out on the city street in rags and sin;
Who'll save the vagrant boy, who'll take him in?

God of the fatherless, gracious and kind,
Thou seest these wandering ones, earth-soiled and blind;
Shepherd of Israel, call to thy fold
These bleating, straying lambs out in the cold.

BROADSTAIRS VILLA,
RAMSDEN R'D,
BALHAM, S. W. }
LONDON, NOV. 21st, 1889.

Dear Madam:—May I ask your acceptance of a little melody which I have composed to accompany your beautiful lines, entitled " It is the Lord," which appeared in *Word and Work* of last May or June? I found the words so sweet and suggestive of recitative measure, that I have ventured to give utterance to my thought as in the enclosed, and trust you will find in it responsive chords, interpreting the verses, which have so deeply touched my heart.

With Christian regard,

Yours in best bonds,

MRS. E. PRIESTLY.

It is the Lord

John xxi; 7.

HEN toiling vainly on the restless tide,
You cast your net upon the " other side,"
And find your draught of fishes multiplied,
  " It is the Lord."

When oft from nights of sorrow you arise,
Greeting the brightness of the morning skies,
Which flood you with a new and glad surprise,
  " It is the Lord."

When you have cast your burdens all aside,
When passion is subdued and self denied,
In the o'ercoming, you have testified,
  " It is the Lord."

When morning dawns upon a night of pain,
And hope replumes your drooping wings again,
And sunshine breaks the spell of cloud and rain,
  " It is the Lord."

When winds have blown some bright-eyed flower to you,
Charged with a cup of fragrance and of dew,
As though the asking of your heart it knew,
  " It is the Lord."

When you have bid the voice of self be still,
And in your earthly lot of good or ill,
From a full heart declare, "Not as I will,"
  " It is the Lord."

When through the valley of the shadow way,
You pass the portal of the glad new day,
Awaking in His likeness, you will say,
  " It is the Lord."

18

George Elliot

ND thou hast joined "the choir invisible,"
Where the "immortal dead live yet again,"
Hast scaled empyrean heights and vaster realms,
And climbed to paths beyond the eagle's ken.
Now, with unclouded vision thou hast looked
Behind the veil of flesh, the spirit's bars;
Hast caught the prospect of a wide expanse,
Through trackless spheres, and galaxy of stars!
Ah! when thine inner vision first beheld,
And knew the fleshly veil drawn full aside,
When what on earth thou only dared to hope,
In its fruition blessed and satisfied,
Methinks, thy fleet-winged steeds did hasten back,
In chariot of fire to earth once more,
With tender ministry to human souls,
Pent in the prison of this earthbound shore.

Through the Mist

YOU must watch for me when the tide comes in,
    And the current sets to shore ;
For my barque will be such a useless thing
    With neither rudder nor oar ;
If you listen to catch what the breezes say
    In the voices of the sea,
You will hear me singing about the " Rock,"
    That was cleft in twain for me.

My hands are too tired to trim the sails,
    Or to ply the needed oar,
So you will not know when my barque drifts in,
    Unless you wait by the shore.
If I cling but to a spar or plank
    Just tossing upon the sea,
You will hear my voice in the shoreward trend,
    " I will hide myself in Thee."

You'll watch for the words may be faint and few
    In the sweet refrain I sing,
But you'll know I'm safe, when you catch the strain,
    To thy cross I simply cling.
I am coming soon for the night has waned,
    And you'll know who calleth me,
When you hear in the dawning still again
    " I will hide myself in Thee."

To My Bible Class

WHILE standing to-day on the border line
    Where the girl and woman meet,
You are culling buds of your morning time,
    With their brimming cups of sweet.

The lavish behests of your childhood's day,
    Which have brought so much to you,
Have filled and o'erfilled your now brimming cup
    With the brightest drops of dew.

But the foam will pass as the days go on,
    And the sun has higher climbed,
And you may not catch as quick a response
    To the bells your dreams have chimed.

The dew will be less, the cup not as full,
    In the coming nooutide heat—
Your paths will not be as smooth and as green
    Nor your lips so full of sweet.

But you need not falter, nor fear to trust,
    The trend of the swelling wave;
Your Pilot is near in storm and in calm,
    And your hearts are strong and brave.

Should the night be dark and the waves so high
    That you cannot hoist a sail,
You can drift, for the current knows the way,
    Though your oar and rudder fail.

The Light of the world, which is pledged to you,
    Shines whitliest in the night,
And you cannot drift, in storm or calm,
    Away from the Father's sight.

Hold fast then the anchor whose stays are cast,
    Far in and behind the vail,
Where your homebound ship will by and by
    Find harbor from wind and gale.

Christmas Eve

DARK fell the night and cold,
Loud shrieked the winds and bold,
Far from its cheerless fold
    One lamb had strayed.
On through the dreary street,
On through the snow and sleet,
On moved the tender feet,
    Where frosts were laid.

Never was face more sad,
Never a heart less glad,
None so unkindly clad,
    So cold and bare.
On from a wretched home,
Her weary feet had come
Fearless of death or gloom,
    Filled with despair.

Vainly she looked to find,
Some place more warm and kind
Than that she'd left behind,
    So desolate.
Houses and homes there are,
Fastened with bolt and bar,
Where not a want may mar,
    Early or late.

Within the sealed walls,
No grief or sorrow falls,
No voice for pity calls,
    No accents wild.
Oft through the shutters tight,
Issue forth gleams of light,
Dazzling the weary sight,
    Of the wan child.

Now by the fitful beam,
Or some delusive dream,
Hope, like a meteor gleam,
    Bade darkness flee.
Clasping with tiny hands,
Frame work of iron bands,
Quick on her tiptoe stands,
    More light to see.

When to her waiting sight
Rose visions of delight,
Quick all the gloomy night,
   Vanished away.
Curtains of crimson fold,
Fastened with bands of gold,
Pendant from windows old,
   Massive and gray.

Light from the frescoed walls,
Through the rich lattice falls,
While through the marble halls,
   Music breathes low.
Tables all running o'er,
With their delicious store,
Cups that were full before,
   Now overflow.

Heads all untouched by care,
Faces divinely fair,
Old age and youth are there—
   Infant and sire.
All this delight I ween,
Little sad eyes have seen,
Looking the bars between,
   At the warm fire.

Colder her hands have grown,
Swiftly the hours have flown,
Now every mirthful tone,
   Dies on her ear.
Once more her frozen feet,
Strive to regain the street,
When hark! what accents sweet
   Banish her fear.

Kind arms thy form enfold,
Come weary one and cold,
Come to the sheltered fold,
   Rest for thee there.
Morning broke cold and gray,
Frozen and still she lay,
No form of polished clay
   More pure and fair.

Transition

IF you were walking in some garden fair
    Or wandering over flowery meads,
With full permission to extract the dews,
    And fill your chalice to its utmost needs,
Would you select the aster robed in state,
    Or from the Passion vine extract the sweet?
Chosing at will some fragrant garden Queen,
    Rather than cull the Daisies at your feet?

Would you not seek in shady nooks to find
    The Lily of the Valley, clothed with grace,
Or wander in the deep'ning shades aside
    Seeking the Blue Bells in their hiding place?
Just so the Master, with a love as kind,
    Searching the borders of your bright parteere,
Has culled your Lily from its hiding place,
    And set its rootlets in His garden fair.

Will it not comfort you sometime to know
    That He whose love so far exceedeth ours,
Has chosen to expand your precious bud
    In the unfolding, with immortal flowers?
If you could wake her as it were from sleep,
    By quickened touch or fondest love confessed,
You would not dare to stir a drifted leaf,
    For fear you might disturb her quiet rest.

You might have held in vain to her frail barque,
    On wilder seas, and on a sweeping tide,
Sometime you might have failed to pilot her,
    'Neath threat'ning skies and on a stream more wide.
The dainty couch which you have spread with care
    Bespeaks the joy of which you are bereft--
The unpressed pillow's snowy drapery
    Needs now no more the touch of fingers deft.

You would not bring again the weary months
    Which held your darling to this bed of pain,
Just to behold her lovely face once more,
    You would not bring the fevered pulse again.
Her last sweet words which you will ne'er forget,
    "I am not dying," were a pledge that she
Knew that the rending of the vail of flesh,
    Would but release and set her spirit free.

She had grown wise and learned in spirit lore,
    Full visioned and full robed in white.—
Like some bright star at the approach of day,
    She paled and faded from your mortal sight.
But you can linger yet a little while
    Waiting and watching 'till the shadows flee—
Knowing that all your blessedness must come
    Through the dark passage of Gethsemine.

White Sulphur Springs

ST. HELENA, CAL.

IKE the enchanted springs of old
  Hid in their mountain rest,
So the famed Sulphurs nestled lie
  Within their rocky nest,
Land-locked by Nature's grand old walls
  And battlements so high,
That oft their domes and minarets
  Lean close against the sky.

The lofty hills reposing on
  Their buttresses so wide
Have drawn their graceful drapery
  Half timidly aside,
And looking from their dizzy heights
  Over the portal wide,
Have sent the cooling, healing stream
  Adown the mountain side.

Fair Switzerland! the land of hills,
  Of mountains and of vales,
Can boast no purer liturgies
  Or more beguiling tales
Than this sweet valley, closely locked
  Within those massive walls,
Where water of perpetual youth
  In endless cadence falls.

Not in the " Happy Valley " of
 The old and classic time,
Did touch of artist or of bard
 Find fairer theme for rhyme
Than this sweet vale, so prodigal
 Of Nature's brimming bowl,
When Nectar and Ambrosia spread
 A feast for heart and soul.

Not Irving's fair " Alhambra " here
 Looms up in massive pride,
But one whose trellised windows 'neath
 Their rustic porches hide—
The " Hermitage " is fairly set
 Against the mountain's side,
Where spirit voices softly chant
 The hymns of eventide.

And " Grape Vine Cottage," quaint and low,
 All redolent of sweet
And old time walls and draperies
 With memories replete.
Then " Sunnyside," with ample hall,
 Stands 'neath the mountain's wing,
Out of whose rocky side there flows
 The *far-famed Sulphur Spring*.

Baby Blue Eyes

BABY, we marvel if your eyes
Set in their depths of blue,
Mirror the heaven of love we bear
Within our hearts for you.
Like lily bells o'ercharged with dew
Which bird and insect sips,
We wait to catch the faintest word
From off your baby lips.

We marvel baby what your thoughts,
And whence your feet have come,
Where is that wonder "Baby Land"
So late your favored home?
The little people which you knew
In that delightful place,
Were they as dainty as our pet,
As sweet and full of grace?

Could they such carol improvise,
Or prattle half so gay,
As our own darling little waif
In charming roundelay?
Your tiny hands and finger tips
As pink as coral shell,
Hold to our lips a draught as cool
As held in lily bell.

Your perfumed breath as full of sweets
As rose or mignonnette,
Is like the fragrance of the flowers
With morning kisses wet—
We could not spare our baby now,
Our precious little girl,
For never could we find again
Another such a pearl.

Like as the tender lambs are borne
Within the shepherd's arms
So Father lead our darling on
Beyond the reach of harms—
Far up the mountain's sunny slopes,
Led by our guileless child,
May we in higher altitudes
Grow pure and undefiled.

Whence and Whither

SOMEBODY'S bark is let loose on the tide,
Somebody's vista is opening wide,
Some one is making the port of success,
Others have hoisted the flag of distress.
Somebody's just girded up for the strife,
Others are yielding the battle of life.
Dews of the morning brushed from the flowers,
Somebody's buds are culled from the bowers.
The sun has gone down with one before noon,
Other one's harvest has ripened too soon.
Somebody's baby has opened its eyes,
Under the light of roseate skies.
Somebody's morning is dawning to-day,
Somebody's feet have just entered the fray.
Somebody's hands have been stained which we know,
Once were as pure and white as the snow.
Hearts have been plighted, hands have been joined,
Somebody's love into gold has been coined.
Vows that are meaningless some one has said,
Some one whose feet to the altar are led.
Some one has launched on the mystical tide,
Husband and wife, bridegroom and bride,
God grant these voyagers somewhere to find,
Out of the region of storm and of wind,
Loves that are no more the sport of the hour,
Buds that mature in the fully robed flower,
Where, all unstained in a world unlike this,

29

Hearts will unite in a union of bliss,
Somebody's children cradled in blight,
Open their eyes in the damps of the night;
Pitiful places for souls to be born,
Robbed of their birthright, hopeless, forlorn.
Someone reclines on cushions of down,
Bearing no cross, seeking no crown:
Only a pallet of straw cradles one—
One more unfortunate under the sun.
Many have mounted the ladder so high,
Round after round till it touches the sky;
Just one more step and their feet will pass through
Out of the old life into the new.
Somebody's feet have been tripped in their flight,
Out of the shadows and darkness of night.
Others have entered the portals of peace,
Chanting their anthems of joyful release.
God grant we may, when the years have grown old,
Enter the gates of the City of Gold.
That not only some one, but all, may come in,
Out of their conflicts, temptations and sin.
Out of the heartaches, the losses, the strife,
Into the rest of the City of Life.

San Bruno

Suggested by an ivory bust of San Bruno, the original of which is in
the Church of Santa Maria degli Angeli in Rome. One of the great
scholars of the Church was wont to say: " If it were not against the rule of
his order he would speak."

IN vision of "Sir Launfal," prayer
　　Was naught, of no avail,
Until in sacrifice of self
　　He found the "Holy Grail."

When late in Classic Rome we reached
　　A consecrated shrine,
And knelt in reverence before
　　A presence felt divine,
It seemed as though the thought of God,
　　Filled the deep silence round,
Voicing Himself through saintly lips
　　In sanctity profound,

Deep in the shrine San Bruno looked
　　The very soul of prayer,
Sweetly the "Benedictus" soft
　　Seemed ringing in the air.
Our Mecca reached, the "Holy Grail"
　　Was but the flesh denied—
The selfhood lost for aye, in God,
　　And Christ, the crucified.

For the Night Cometh

H, can you not be patient while you may,
When you have such a little while to stay?
You may repress that tear or rising sigh
Just for the joy that cometh by-and-by,
When you will know the how and why.

The dear fond hearts held close within our own,
The voice that greets us with confiding tone,
Will not be your behest or mine alway.
Oh, let us then be loving while we may,
We have so little while to stay.

What if the lips which have defended you
From accusation rude, unkind, untrue,
Should some time hesitate or blindly miss
The recognition of a word or kiss,
And so should seem to you to go amiss.

Can you misjudge or question all the years
Just for the poor indulgence of your fears?
Oh, these same faults will some day seem as naught,
Only as strange, odd ways with kindness fraught,
Which care for you has taught.

The feet which to your own have timed their tread,
Fain to keep pace in paths where you have led
Have tripped or may be fallen by the way,
Alas! they have so little while to stay,
Forgive and help them while you may.

Dear, precious hands which oft have smoothed your
      brow,
They were not once as hard of touch as now;
  But they are still fond hands and clean, you know,
  Though seeming many times too fast or slow,
  They are still whiter than the snow.

Dear heart, with impulse ever warm and true,
Full of fond thoughts and tender love for you,
  What if the flood-tide of some fevered beat
  Time not to words which you would deem most mete,
  In benedictions soft and sweet?

When the dear hearts are cold within each breast,
And friends we love have entered into rest,
  We will not think their feet were once too slow
  In the same path where now in tears and woe
  Alone and silently we go.

Odors, Whence Come They?

I'M thinking to-day of a white rosebud
  We placed on our baby's breast,
As he lay in the silence white and still,
  Like a sleeping child at rest.
'Twas only an op'ning bud, we had
  Culled from the children's bower,
But before the little casket was closed
  It came to a perfect flower.

The odor which made my spirit so faint
  In that time of sighs and tears,
Cometh now, as then, with a touch of pain
  Adown through the waste of years—
And one precious child half-grown to a man,
  Weaves about me a tender spell,
With odor of Pinks and Mignonettes,
  Which he knew I loved so well.

One dear little daughter, with eyes as blue
  As azure of summer skies,
Comes with the wild flowers weighting her hands,
  And the love light in her eyes.
      *   *   *   *   *   *
Ah, the subtle spell which perfumes entwine
  About us where'er we go,
In the stir of garments, and presence sweet,
  Of the angels whom we know,
Is like to the breath of Him, who declared
  When He knew He could not stay,
" I will send you the Comforter, because
  For a while I go away."

Greeting

Sent by request from Napa, Cal., to the Y. M. C. A. of Fall River, Mass.

YOU question if the tale be true,
    If 'tis not overtold,
That earth's best gifts do so enrich
    Our sunset land of gold?

    Could touch of artist improvise
        A portraiture for me,
    I'd send in panoramic views
        My answer o'er the sea.

    Like fairy pictures you would find
        O'erarched by heaven's dome,
    Scenes of enchantment which begird
        My own sweet valley home.

    Nestled 'neath mountain ranges, where
        Birds of bright plumage fly,
    O'ertopped by nature's minarets
        Our homes and temples lie.

    Flowers which you rear with tender care
        Need here no training hand,
    Mosses and ferns and blossoms wild
        Carpet the fragrant land.

    Perennial streams and fountains cool
        Lodged in the mountain side,
    Send down their sparkling healing streams
        Into the valley wide.

Old oaks magnificent and tall
  Broad canopies of shade
Have stood for centuries, nor feared
  The stroke of vandal blade.

Whole palaces in air sweep by,
  With windows all aglow!
With banquets of delight for those
  Gazing from plains below.

Oh, then when summer days again
  Their symphonies prolong,
Come to our hill environed home
  And learn its fabled song.

OUR ANSWER

FROM MRS. MARY B. C. SLADE,

Editor "Children's Hour"
Fall River, Mass.

Sweet friend, so near, so far away,
Your thousand friends all bid me say,
We'll come, if you will "name the day."
We know your heart has ample room,
But what if all the crowd should come
And overfill your valley home?
I know your wit would build a stair
To reach those " palaces in air,"
And hold your feast of welcome there.
We'll go to see you, soon or late:
Watch for us Mary, watch and wait,
At the Golden—or the Pearly gate.

"From the Grave of Keats"

LIKE pilgrims at some wayside shrine we met,
  She drew me to a sparkling fountain near,
Holding a brimming cup for me to drink,
  We quaffed together of the water clear.

Anon! she greeted me from foreign shores,
  O'er land and sea her message reached my home.
A few rare flowers from the grave of Keats,
  She kindly culled for me in classic Rome.

And now she greets me from a foreign shore
  Along whose banks entwine the immortelles,
And where she proffers me again a cup
  Filled from the water of eternal wells.

Sweet spirit send this oft repeated draught
  My yearning and my fevered thirst to stay.
That I may stand white-robed and beautiful,
  In the near closing of my earthly day.

Two Sleeping Cities

SAN FRANCISCO AND LONE MOUNTAIN

BOTH looking seaward catch the inborne tide,
Both woo the ripples which to landward glide ;
Both hold their sleepers through the silent night,
Softly enwrapped in drapery of white.

Both stretch their borders broader and more broad,
Both lie beneath the watchful eye of God ;
On velvet couches or neath prison bars,
Their sleepers lie under the dome of stars.

Yet *one* wakes not at touch of early morn ;
It hath no enterprise of sunrise born ;
No touch of life or tread of busy feet
Along the long drawn aisles and silent street.

Under the ivied archways hewn in stone,
Beneath the marbles standing cold and lone,
No pilgrim or sojourner breaks the spell,
Voicing the silence, save that "all is well."

A stillness as of hearts which no more beat,
Which no more quicken at the sound of feet ;
No pulsing life by hope or duty led
Voices the city of the sleeping dead.

The silences which hold the sleepers here,
Have no remorseful agonies, no dread or fear,
No sullen discontent or hopeless grief,
Craving the boon that death may bring relief.

Hard by these resting ones with folded hands,
The sleeping city of the living stands :
With voices hushed and tired limbs laid down,
They reck no more of crosses or of crown.

38

The babe pressed fondly to its mother's heart,
Knows not the maelstorm in the city's mart,
Nestled so softly in the warm home nest,
It sleeps the sleep of innocence most blest.

But one dear child is missing from the home,
Whose feet have learned in doubtful paths to roam,
One darling boy, so late his father's pride
Has launched his barque on the returnless tide.

The midnight hour finds him with ready feet,
Roaming with careless tread the city's street;
He heeds not now his mother's cry of pain,
Calling him back to love and home again.

The darling of her heart, in hours belate,
Stands just a moment at the fatal gate;
The dazzling light and revelry within,
Tempt him to take one look at crime and sin,

Great God! the trap is sprung; the boy distraught,
Within the ready snare is quickly caught;
He dallied like the moth about the flame,
Till drawn within a den of sin and shame.

One more unfortunate has found the snare
Set for unwary feet with skillful care;
This mother's darling, half in love with sin,
With half reluctant step was drawn within.

Hard by the seething palpitating heat,
The watchman makes his oft repeated beat;
He recks not that the fatal trap is sprung,
And one more victim from the noose is swung.

His eyes familiar with the sick'ning sight,
Heed not the horrors of the fatal night;
Would God our precious boys to ruin led
Were safe within the city of the dead.

A Denial

NOT we, made one with the Father through Christ,
　　Do fade as fadeth the leaf,
No more than the grain of the wheat is lost
　　In winnowing of the sheaf.

No more than the butterfly, once released
　　From its narrow, darkened cell,
Can linger around the deserted walls
　　Of a hollow, broken shell.

Ah, who would remain in the chrysalis,
　　In the dawning of the light—
With the soul set free from the walls of sense,
　　Full poised for freedom and flight?

As the leaves fade, so this garment of flesh
　　Drops off when its work is done,—
So the Old Year casts by its faded robes
　　When the New Year is begun.

And the soul, thank God, bursts its bars of flesh,
　　With the heavens full in sight!
It breaks away from the shadows of sense—
　　On the wings of endless flight!

So man, redeemed, on the pinions of faith,
　　Goes forth in a realm more broad;
While finding the gift of Eternal Life,
　　Is the self hood lost in God.

My Rose Tree

A ROSE tree grown in my lovely parterre
So gracefully leans on the morning air,
It seems a vision of beauty there.

Down in the silences, hidden away,
Under the sod, curtained from day,
The mother roots of my rose tree stay.

Eight grafts I gave to her motherly care,
Which shared with her own the sunlight and air,
And grew into grace wondrously fair!

Waiting, a marvel of beauty beheld!
Out of the Darkness, shadow and cold
Cometh my buds of Ophir and Gold,

The mother of nine! what rapture to tell!
Her roses that bloom in their love-sheltered dell
Like dream flowers seem, or fair immortelle.

Speechless with wonder and gladness, I see
Hung from the boughs of my lovely rose tree,
The typical nine in units of three!

In silence too deep and grateful for speech,
I cull of my roses just within reach,
And learn the lessons of wisdom they teach.

The fond mother tree in accents divine,
Tenderly greeteth her beautiful nine!
"Ye are the branches, I am the vine."

41

"What Will Remain?"

WITHIN his palace walls the King lay dying,
　　Soft lights and perfumed airs flooded the room,
The far-spent fevered threads of life were flying
　　Swift through the closing loom.

Just as the shadows with the dawn were blending,
　　The King looked up and beckoned with his hand
The faithful watchers at his couch attending,
　　Who waited his command.

"Bear ye my winding sheet with measured marches,
　　It is the only garment left your King;
Through busy streets and under templed arches,
　　Its narrow foldings fling."

Say, "it is all now left of crown and treasure,
　　Of kingdom, pageantries, of long sought gains,
Of earthly good which seemed an over measure;
　　A pall! all that remains."

When we have tried all that there is in living,
　　E'en to the uttermost, the very best,
What will remain of all earth's vaunted giving,
　　What but the soul's unrest?

Ah, in the time of finished work and resting,
　　When nothing but things real count for gains,
May, what will bear the crucial work of testing,
　　Be to us, what remains.

Easter Lillies

AUSPICIOUS morn! Adown the East
    Thy gates of Light unfold!
Sunrise o'ertops the mountain heights
    In flooding tides of gold.
        Our waking eyes
        Glad with surprise,
    New glories now behold!

Oh, day of days! Oh, morn of morns!
    Crown of the newborn year,
The risen Christ has chased the gloom
    From sorrow's night of fear.
        The shadows flee,
        Lifted by Thee,
    The dawning draweth near.

The voices of the forest sing
    A matin sweet and low,
Their sacramental liturgies
    On wind harps come and go.
        These Easter days
        Of song and praise,
    In tides of worship flow.

The blue-eyed Gentian lifteth up
    Her modest smiling face,
Where frosts of winter could not hide
    Or mar her spring time grace.
        Bid to arise
        Her sweet blue eyes,
    Are beaming with surprise.

While walking through the forest snows
  You sometimes stay your feet,
Lest an untimely tread may crush
  Some hidden woodland sweet,
    It does not seem
    That frosts which gleam,
Were late its winding sheet.

Perchance you did not think of this
  Bright resurrection morn!
When finding underneath your feet
  This Child of beauty born.
    You did not see
    How gracefully,
Her chrismal robes were worn.

Your Easter lillies which have been
  Unfolding through the snows.
Herald in their prophetic type
  The morn our Saviour rose,
    With conquest wide ·
    The Crucified
Has conquered all our foes.

Oh, day of days! Oh, morn of morns!
  Crown of the newborn year,
The risen Christ has chased the gloom
  From sorrow's night of fear.
    The shadows flee
    Lifted by Thee,
The dawning draweth near.

Foresplendors

IN the deep stillness of the early morning,
    When darkness flees and shadows pass away,
My soul awakes into the perfect dawning,
    In the foresplendors which around me play!

Refreshed and strengthened by a night of resting,
    My spirit poises for a nobler flight,
Like as a bird new fledged from out her nesting,
    Mounts ever skyward in the quicking light.

So the New Year awakened from the sleeping
    Of the Old Year, now passed beyond our sight,
Will in the morning of its precious reaping,
    Bring in the sheaves it gathered in the night.

The glad New Year forecast the life immortal,
    Where Thou, oh Father, bidst the shadows flee!
When passing in behind the shining portal,
    We shall awake and find ourselves with Thee.

By Still Waters

LIKE as the hart with fevered lips
  Seeketh the shady nooks,
Panting and leaping at the sound
  Of flowing water brooks.

So thou my soul in searching through
  The universe abroad,
Art hungry for the bread of life
  And thirsty for thy God.

Oft as kind nature broodeth o'er
  The shepherd with his sheep,
Wooing them to her fond embrace
  In sweet, refreshing sleep.

So thou, Oh, Father ! givest to
  Thy children waking dreams
Of that blest Eden, where the soul
  Quaffs from eternal streams.

Oft in some pressing need of life
  My cup is over-filled,
When on my soul the cooling dews
  Of heaven are distilled.

And in the lull of water brooks
  I slake my thirst at length,—
While to some other fevered lips,
  I hold my cup of strength.

Only the Baby

HO says " 'Tis only the baby that died?"
Only *she*, the wee lamb of our fold—
Only *her* little eye-lids have closed on the light,
Only *her* little hands have grown cold.

Only dear little Will, or Ida, or Grace,
Or she who had no name but *pet*—
How trifling a sorrow, how easy 'twill be
The tender blue eyes to forget.

How often we hear it, how coldly it sounds
On the ear of the mother who weeps—
Only her little nestling, her tiniest one,
Only baby, dear baby, that sleeps.

Only baby! alas, how blindly 'tis said—
'Tis the bud that grows nearest the heart,
Its tendrils twine closest, most lovingly too,
So hard from the life-stem to part.

Know ye not, that the lamp of our love has gone out,
That music has ceased in our home,
That the trilling so soft, so bewitchingly sweet,
Echoes not, since our *birdling* has flown?

Oh, say not, " 'Tis only the baby that died,"
There is nothing in life half so dear--
'Tis the magnet which draws our soul to the skies,
And brings us to *heaven* so near.

Ad Finem

THOUGH years now gone seem but a waste,
 Oh! Thou who gavest me
So much of good and blessedness
 To hold in trust for Thee,

Though what I might have been, demands
 A wherefore now, and why ?
And I have nought to answer Thee
 But a regretful sigh ;

Is it too late, at eventide,
 To do some work for Thee?
Some sacrifice of self to make?
 Some captive to set free?

Too late to quench some fevered thirst,
 Or tide of sin to stay?
To save some soul distraught with fear
 From peril and dismay?

I would not care to enter heaven,
 Wherever that may be,
If far behind I saw adrift
 Some helpless barque at sea—

Sooner would I go back and launch
 A life-boat on the tide,
And bring the storm-tossed safely in,
 Though heaven were long denied.

But if 'tis mine to enter there,
 All I may dare to ask
Is just to sit low at Thy feet
 And ply the humblest task.

If in Thy vast domain I find
 Some place allotted me,
Oh! send me back to earth again
 On love's sweet ministry.